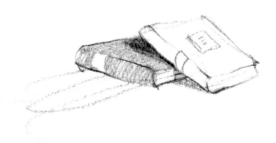

First published in English in 2016 by Peter Pauper Press, Inc.
English translation by Mara Lethem

Originally published in Spain as *La muntanya de llibres més alta del món*
Text and illustrations © 2015 by Rocio Bonilla
© Edicions Bromera, S. L. Alzira, 2015. www.bromera.com

Published by Peter Pauper Press, Inc.
202 Mamaroneck Avenue
White Plains, New York 10601
U.S.A.

Published in the United Kingdom and Europe by Peter Pauper Press, Inc.
c/o White Pebble International
Unit 2, Plot 11 Terminus Rd.
Chichester, West Sussex PO19 8TX, UK

Library of Congress Cataloging-in-Publication Data

Names: Bonilla, Rocio, 1970- author, illustrator. | Lethem, Mara, translator.
Title: The highest mountain of books in the world / Rocio Bonilla ; English
    translation by Mara Lethem.
Other titles: Muntanya de llibres més alta del món. English
Description: White Plains, New York : Peter Pauper Press, Inc., 2016. |
    Originally published in Spain by Edicions Bromera in 2015 under title:
    La muntanya de llibres més alta del món. | Summary: A boy who wants to fly
    discovers the many ways that books can take him to the greatest heights.
Identifiers: LCCN 2015043060 | ISBN 9781441319999 (hardcover : alk. paper)
Subjects: | CYAC: Books and reading--Fiction. | Flight--Fiction. |
    Imagination--Fiction.
Classification: LCC PZ7.1.B669 Hi 2016 | DDC [E]--dc23 LC record available at
https://lccn.loc.gov/2015043060

ISBN 978-1-4413-1999-9
Manufactured for Peter Pauper Press, Inc.
Printed in Hong Kong

7 6 5 4 3 2

Visit us at www.peterpauper.com

THE HIGHEST MOUNTAIN OF BOOKS IN THE WORLD

Rocio Bonilla

PETER PAUPER PRESS, INC.
WHITE PLAINS, NEW YORK

For my mom,
who was the life and soul of the house,
for paps,
our guardian angel,
and for Ruth,
my little Bruce Lee

THE HIGHEST MOUNTAIN
OF BOOKS IN THE WORLD

Rocio Bonilla

Lucas was convinced
he was born to fly.

He could spend hours watching the birds soar
or airplanes leaving white trails in the sky up above.

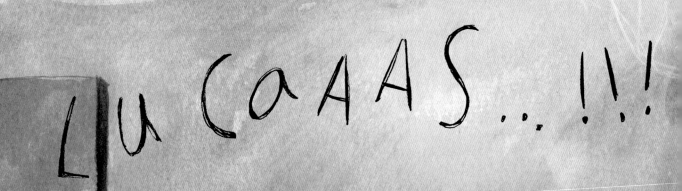

LuCaAAS...!!!

He tried to make wings many times—
millions of wings.
Big ones, small ones, even ones with real feathers.

Surely, he thought, one of his inventions
would make his dream come true ... *to fly!*
But none did.

Santa Claus,

. . .

Lucas refused to give up.

Every Christmas he would write Santa Claus a letter asking him to "pretty, pretty please bring me wings that can really fly."

But for some reason, year after year, Santa got it wrong, giving him toy wings that were no use at all.

On his birthday, after blowing out the candles on his cake
and making the same wish he'd made
each and every birthday before, his mother said,
"There are other ways to fly, Lucas."

And she put a book in his hands.

At first, Lucas didn't understand what she meant,
but he sat in the garden and started to read anyway.

He loved the story that his mother had given him so much,
he finished it in one sitting.

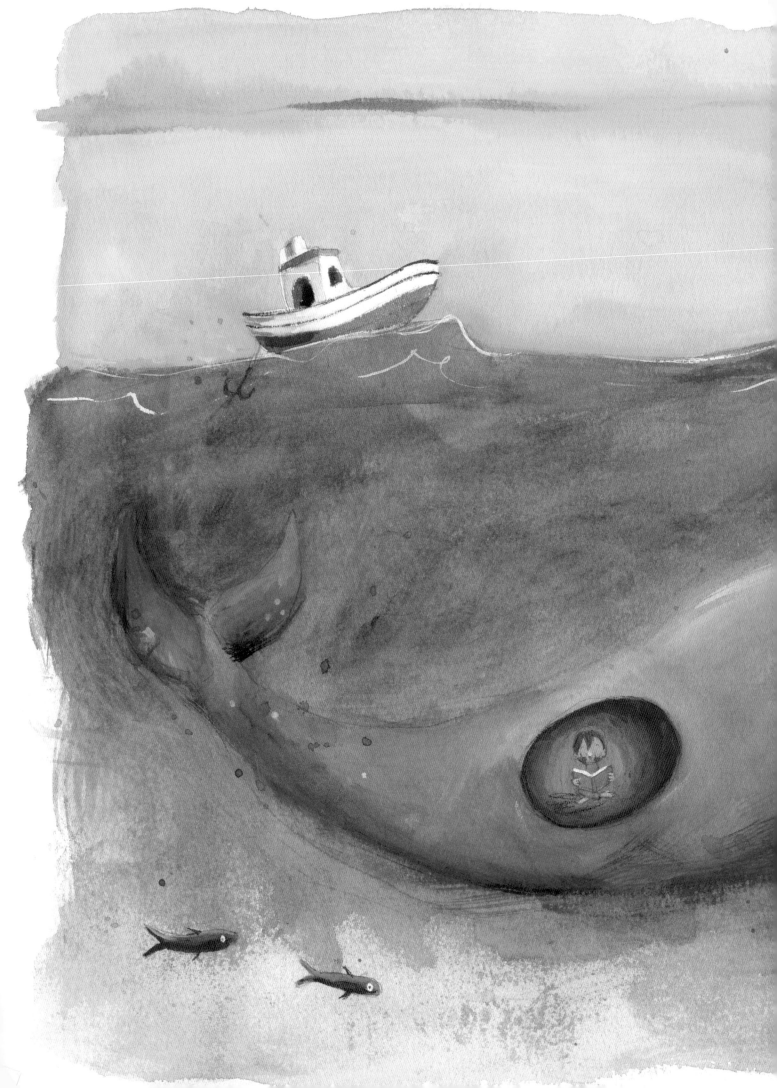

Almost without realizing it, he picked up another book . . .
and then another . . . and another.

He was amazed by everything he discovered,
learned, and imagined.

He started to devour books endlessly,
and the more he read, the faster he read.

He couldn't stop.

He soon finished all the books from the bookcase in the living room,
and the books from his sister's room, too.

Before he knew it, the garden was full of books.
He stacked them up, sat on them, and asked for more.

Everyone brought him books:
his best friend, Thomas, the girl next door, . . .

. . . the music teacher, his grandfather,
and even the local baker.

And so, his mountain of books grew and grew and grew.
After a while, Lucas stopped coming down—
not even to eat or sleep.

His mother, his sister, and even the fire department
tried to get him to come down,
but Lucas could only think about reading.

When he had finished all the books in the neighborhood,
he started on vans full of books from the local library.
The mountain of books grew higher, and he became so famous
that he was even on TV.

When people found out about him they came from all over

THE HIGHEST
MOUNTAIN OF BOOKS
IN THE WORLD

to see the highest mountain of books in the world.

Lucas didn't notice anything. He just kept on reading.

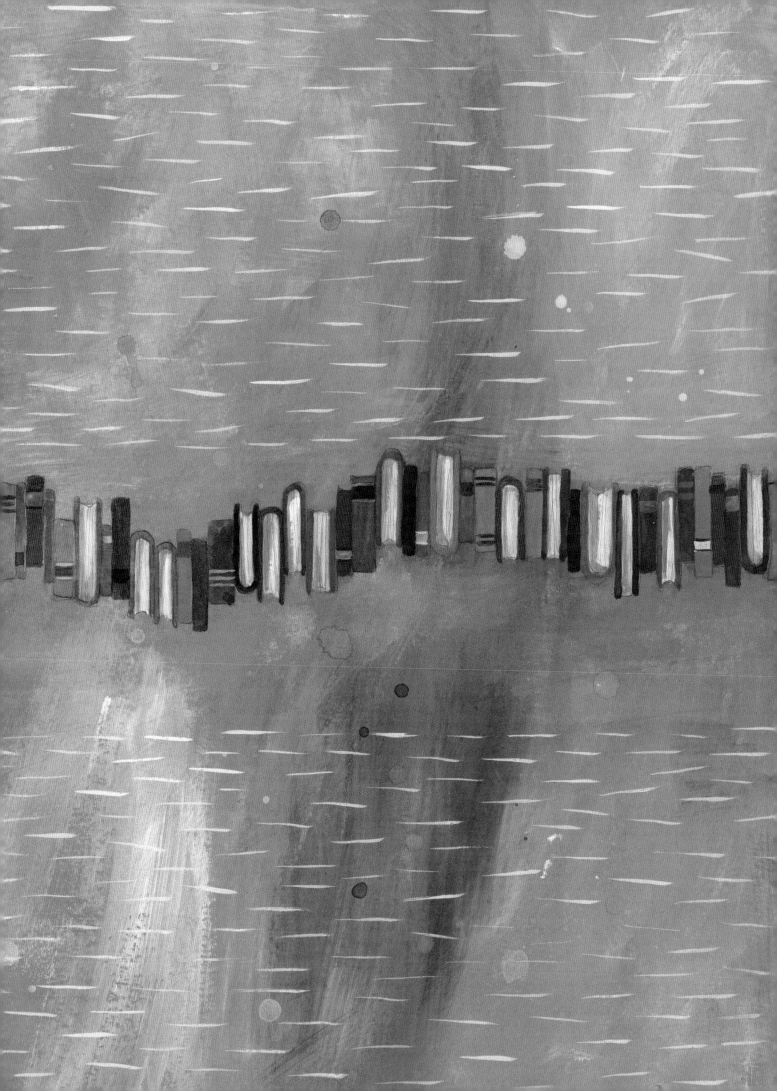

With each story, he traveled to other countries, discovered interesting things about history, met new characters, and imagined worlds that didn't really exist.

And then one day, all of sudden . . .
he understood what his mother meant!

Even though he couldn't fly, his imagination could.
In fact, he realized that he hadn't stopped flying
since he'd started his first book.

And at that moment he wanted to climb down the mountain
to tell her.

But . . . how?

And that's when his imagination allowed him to fly . . . yet once again.